Kim's Top Hat

Diane Marwood

W
FRANKLIN WATTS
LONDON•SYDNEY

Designer: Matthew Lilly

Printed in China

...nd Pesky Ltd.

Franklin Watts is a division of
Hachette Children's Books,
an Hachette UK company.

... Espresso characters are the property of
Espresso Education Ltd.

www.hachette.co.uk

Level 1 50 words
Concentrating on CVC words plus and, the, to

Level 2 70 words
Concentrating on double letter sounds and new letter
sounds (ck, ff, ll, ss, j, v, w, x, y, z, zz) plus no, go, I

Level 3 100 words
Concentrating on new graphemes (qu, ch, sh, th, ng,
ai, ee, igh, oa, oo, ar, or, ur, ow, oi, ear, air, ure, er)
plus he, she, we, me, be, was, my, you, they, her, all

Level 4 150 words
Concentrating on adjacent consonants (CVCC/CCVC
words) plus said, so, have, like, some, come, were, there,
little, one, do, when, out, what

Kim got a top hat.

In the top hat, Kim got a pen.

In the top hat,
Kim got a mug.

In the top hat, Kim got a rat.

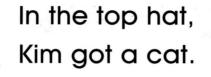

In the top hat,
Kim got a cat.

In the top hat, Kim got Sal.

In the top hat, Kim got... Dad!

Kim got in
the top hat!

12

Puzzle Time

Match the words that rhyme
to the pictures!

bad

dim

hat

hug

him

Dad

Tim

mug

sad

rug

mat

Kim

sat

Answers

hat – mat, sat   **mug** – hug, rug

Dad – bad, sad   **Kim** – dim, him, Tim

Espresso Connections

This book may be used in conjunction with the Literacy area on Espresso to secure children's phonics learning. Here are some suggestions.

Word Machine

Encourage children to play the Word Machine Level 1. Demonstrate how the machine works, and then move on to the activities.

Ask children to find the correct first letter.
Then ask children to find the correct last letter.
Then ask children to find the correct middle letter.

Check that children are able to hear the difference between the letter sounds as different words come up.

Praise plausible attempts, such as substituting the letter "k" for "c" when attempting to find the hard c sound.

Finally, ask children to find all the letters of the word.

Spot the Word

Choose a book from the Big Book selection, for example **"Places we like to visit"** to play Spot the Word.

Give children pieces of paper with the high frequency words **and** or **the** or **to**. (The class could be split, with groups of children looking for different words.)

Ask children to note down on the paper each time they have seen or heard the word they are looking for.

At the end of the book, children should count up how many times their target word has been used.

Go back through the book together and see whether they got it right.

Praise plausible attempts, for example "they" for "the" and take the opportunity to point out why these words are different.

You could replicate the activity with this phonics story.